Contents

Chapter 1
A Poor Orphan

Long, long ago, the people who lived close to the Tatra Mountains of Poland were ruled by Duke Edmund. The Duke was a mean, greedy man. Every year, at harvest time, he left his castle, and rode out with his soldiers to collect rents and taxes from the poor.

One year, the Duke and his men went to the farm of a man called Tomas, who lived with his wife Rosa and their little boy

Janosik. The three of them went out to meet the Duke in the yard outside their home.

Duke Edmund did not get down from his horse. "Where is the rent you owe me?" he asked Tomas.

Tomas shook with fear. "The summer was too hot and dry, my lord," he said. "My crops did not grow. I have no money to pay your rent, but I promise that I will pay you double next year."

"Your promises are of no use to me!" shouted the Duke. He turned to his chief soldier. "Captain, hang this man from that tree over there. Turn the woman and the brat out of the house. I'll rent the farm to someone else."

Tomas begged for mercy, but Duke Edmund had already ridden away. He didn't even turn round.

Janosik was too young to do anything to help. He could only watch the soldiers do their work. They hung his father from the tree with a rope round his neck. Janosik watched him die, writhing, turning this way and that and twitching. Rosa fell to her knees, howling in misery.

Janosik and his mother had nowhere to go. The soldiers took their farm. They had to walk from village to village, begging for food and shelter. In the winter, hunger and sorrow drove Rosa mad, then she became ill with a fever and died. Janosik couldn't dig a grave to bury her. No one would lend him a shovel, and the ground was frozen too hard for him to dig a grave with his bare hands. He had to leave her in a ditch.

In the spring, Janosik went into the mountains. He taught himself how to hunt, and learned which roots and berries were good to eat. As the years passed and he

became older, Janosik grew to love the mountains, and he knew their secret places better than anyone. He spent so much time in the open, he almost forgot that he had ever lived in a house. But Janosik never forgot his mother and father. Because of what happened to them, he hated all soldiers, and he hated Duke Edmund even more.

"One day, I'll get my own back on the Duke. I'll have my revenge," Janosik often promised himself, though he did not know what his revenge would be, or how he would take it.

Early one morning in autumn, when Janosik was 16, he was climbing a steep path high in the mountains. The path became more and more narrow, until it was no more than a rocky ledge on the side of a cliff.

Janosik heard a screech, and saw an eagle glide past.

"If I had wings like yours, my friend, I would fly far away to a better life," Janosik said.

Just in front of him, the path turned left into a gap between two big stones. All at once three men came through the gap, walking one after the other. The first two men were soldiers, with swords in their belts. Behind them was a plump man, dressed in fine clothes.

The first soldier frowned at Janosik. "You're in my master's way, peasant," he said. "Turn around, and go back to a place where the path is wide enough for us to pass each other."

Janosik did not like being told what to do. "I'm not turning back!" he said.

The plump man's face went red with anger. "Do as you are told, peasant!" he shouted. "You don't know how important

I am. My name is Lord Grigor. I am a close friend of Duke Edmund's."

"I don't care who you are," said Janosik. "I'm not turning back."

"I've wasted enough time on you!" yelled Lord Grigor. "Guards, kill him!"

Chapter 2
The Fight

The first soldier reached for his sword. Before he could pull it out, Janosik grabbed him, and threw him down the mountainside. The man fell screaming, until his skull smashed against a rock below.

The second soldier had his sword out ready, and he swung it at Janosik's head. Janosik ducked down and rammed his shoulder into the guard's body. The guard lost his balance. He fell to his death, and his corpse joined the broken, bleeding body of his friend on the rocks below.

Lord Grigor shook in fear. "Please don't kill me!" he begged. "Look, I have money! I will give it to you if you let me live." He took a fat purse from his belt, and held it out to Janosik.

Janosik took the purse. At the same moment, Lord Grigor pulled out a dagger

with his other hand, and tried to stab Janosik in the heart.

Janosik twisted sideways so that the dagger missed him. Then he broke Lord Grigor's nose with a single punch.

Lord Grigor grunted in pain. He fell backwards, tripped over a stone, and tumbled to his death on the rocks far below.

Janosik stopped to get his breath back, then opened the purse and looked inside. It was stuffed with gold coins.

This money comes from the high rents Lord Grigor makes his farmers pay him, Janosik told himself. *How many children went without food to fill this purse? How many families lost their homes?*

Janosik had an idea that made him smile. "I'm not going to keep this gold for myself!" he said out loud. "I'm going to give it back to the people Lord Grigor took it from. That will be how I pay Duke Edmund back. I will steal money from him and his friends, and give it to the poor!"

Janosik walked down the path, filled with excitement. He did not know that he was being spied on. Hidden eyes had watched his every move, and every word he'd said had been listened to.

Chapter 3
The Test

Over the next weeks, Janosik became famous. He robbed many rich travellers on their way across the mountains, and gave their money away to the people who needed it most. Janosik was a hero to the poor, and everywhere he went, they greeted him with smiles and cheers.

Duke Edmund was afraid of Janosik, and he hated him. He put up posters, to tell everyone that Janosik was an outlaw. Anyone

who helped him would be put to death, but if anyone betrayed him and told Duke Edmund where to find Janosik, they'd get a big reward. The Duke sent out soldiers with tracker dogs to hunt Janosik down. But Janosik hid deeper and deeper in the mountains, in places where not even he had been before.

One wild winter night, a troop of soldiers almost took Janosik prisoner in an inn. Janosik was lucky. He escaped out of a back window, and then climbed up a mountain in a roaring blizzard. Snowflakes filled his eyes, and made it difficult to see. The wind was so strong that he had to cling to rocks to keep himself from being blown away. Janosik had not eaten for two days, and he was worn out. Half-way up the mountain, he didn't think he'd be able to carry on. Above the noise of the wind, he could hear the voices of the soldiers who were following him, and the barking of their dogs.

"I have two choices," Janosik said to himself. "I can either hand myself in to the soldiers and be hung, or hide somewhere and die of cold."

He pushed snow out of his eyes, and then stopped in wonder. A little way ahead, firelight glowed in the mouth of a cave. Janosik crawled over to the cave, and fell inside. He saw three lovely young maidens standing around a cooking pot that steamed and bubbled over a coal fire. One maiden was fair, one was dark, and the third had red hair.

"Come closer, Janosik," said the fair maiden. "Warm yourself by our fire."

Janosik gasped. "How did you know my name?" he asked.

The dark maiden answered him. "We know all about you," she said. "We have been following you since the day you fought with Lord Grigor and his men."

Janosik was puzzled. "But that's impossible!" he said. "If you had followed me, how is it that I never saw you? You must be witches!"

The red-haired maiden smiled. "Do not be afraid, Janosik," she said. "We do have magical powers but we are not witches. We are the Spirits of the Tatra Mountains. Our magic will protect you. The soldiers and dogs who are chasing you will not even see this cave."

The fair maiden dropped something into the cooking pot, and its steam turned blue. "Tell us," she said, "if we use our magic to make you the best thief in the world, what will you do? Will you make yourself richer than Duke Edmund?"

"No!" replied Janosik. "I'll give the money to poor people."

"First, we need to be sure that you deserve our help," said the dark maiden. "We will test how strong and how brave you are. But be warned! If you make even the smallest sound or movement when we test you, we will vanish, and you will freeze to death in this cave."

Janosik laughed. "Then I have nothing to lose!" he said. "If I fail, I'll be no worse off than I was before. I'm ready, let the test begin."

The maidens began to sing a weird song, and their voices rang out around the cave. They lifted their hands above their heads, and as they did, a red-hot coal flew out of the fire, and stuck to Janosik's chest. Smoke rose from his burning clothes, and then Janosik felt a terrible pain as the coal sizzled on his skin.

Chapter 4
The Gifts

The pain was almost too much to bear. Janosik was afraid that he might faint, but he remembered what the maidens had told him. He kept silent and still. Sweat ran down his face. He could smell his own flesh burning, and it made him feel sick.

At last, the maidens let their arms drop and their singing stopped. The coal fell back into the fire, and the pain on Janosik's chest went away. He sighed with relief.

19

"You have done well, Janosik," the fair maiden told him. "Now each of us will give you a gift that will help you to be a great thief, and a champion of the poor."

The red-haired maiden went to the back of the cave. When she came back she had a folded jacket and shirt, and a pair of boots in her arms. She put them down at Janosik's feet. "These are magic clothes," she told him. "When you wear them, no enemy sword or knife can pierce them, and arrows will bounce off them."

"Thank you for your wonderful gift!" said Janosik.

The dark maiden went to the back of the cave. She returned with a red leather belt, which she put on top of the clothes at Janosik's feet. "This belt is magic," she told him. "When you wear it, you will be able to run so fast that no enemy will be able to keep up with you."

"Thank you for your wonderful gift!" said Janosik.

The fair maiden went to the back of the cave. She returned with a wooden staff, which she gave to Janosik. "With that staff in your hand, you will be a better climber than a mountain goat," she told him. "What is more, you can use the staff to fight with, for it can hit out quicker than you can think."

"How can I repay you all for these gifts?" said Janosik.

The three maidens spoke at the same time. "Repay us by using them wisely," they said, and they slowly vanished away into empty shadows.

Janosik changed into his new clothes. He put on the red belt, and then looked round the cave for something to eat. In a dark corner, he found a shelf carved into the rock. On the shelf stood a loaf of bread, a small cheese, and a bottle of wine. Janosik took them, and ate and drank his fill. Then he settled down beside the fire, and soon fell asleep.

Chapter 5
Ambush!

Early the next morning, Janosik left the cave. Nowhere could he see the soldiers and dogs who had been hunting him the night before. He guessed that the snow-storm had driven them back.

The weather was fine. The sunshine was bright on the snow-drifts that the wind had made in the night. Janosik could not wait to try out his new powers, and he set off up the mountain.

He was amazed to see how fast he went. His feet stepped so lightly that they left no tracks in the snow. The magic staff led him the shortest and safest way. Janosik laughed out loud. The sound of his laughter scared a mountain hare. The hare ran off. Janosik raced after it, and overtook it. "This is more like flying than running!" he said to himself.

Janosik walked right up to the top of the mountain, and then went down into the valley that lay on the other side. Before long, he entered a dark forest of pine trees. There was only one track, so Janosik went along it, whistling a cheerful tune. Suddenly, a band of men with clubs and knives rushed out from behind some trees and surrounded him.

One of the men was enormous. He had a bushy brown beard, and a scar on one cheek. "It looks as if our luck has changed for the better, lads!" he said with a nasty laugh.

"We've caught a fine rich gentleman this time."

Janosik looked the big man right in the eyes. "You are mistaken, my friend," he said. "I have no money. I am as poor as you are."

"Poor?" said the big man. "You can't be poor with clothes like that. Take them off! We'll sell them for good money at a village market. Hand over that staff of yours as well."

Janosik stood firm. "If you want my clothes and my staff, you will have to fight me for them," he said.

The big man gave a shrug. "Just as you wish," he said. "Get him, lads!"

As the men closed in, Janosik jumped high into the air. Spinning like a dancer, he stepped onto the top of the men's backs. He swung his staff about with such speed that

their eyes could not follow it. The staff knocked the knives and clubs out of the men's hands. Then it whacked them across their backs and heads until they fell to the ground. There they lay groaning, and rubbing their sore arms and legs.

The big man sat up and shook his head. His face looked grim. "Five men against one, and we get beaten!" he grumbled. "We must be the worst bandits in all of Poland."

"Then why not give up being bandits, and try to earn an honest living instead?" asked Janosik.

"We were honest once," said the big man. "We were all farmers. Then Duke Edmund put up our rents, and drove us off our farms. We have no land and no homes. If we don't steal food and money, our families will starve."

Janosik had an idea. "What's your name?" he said.

"Leon," replied the big man. "What is yours?"

"Janosik," said Janosik.

The bandits stared at one another. Their mouths dropped open. They had heard all about Janosik. Could this really be him?

"Listen, Leon," Janosik went on. "How would you like to feed your families, and get your own back on Duke Edmund at the same time?"

Leon frowned. "Of course we'd like it!" he said. "But how can we?"

"Join up with me," said Janosik. "Let me be your chief and I'll show you the best places in the mountains to ambush rich travellers. We'll take their money, and share it out among the poor."

Leon stood up, and shook Janosik's hands. "Agreed!" he said. "You are our leader now, and we'll be glad to follow you. After all, a man who can fight as well as you, can do anything!"

Chapter 6
In the Forest

Janosik and his men set up a camp in the mountains. From there, they carried out their plans to bring misery to the rich, and joy to the poor. All over Poland, people heard the stories about Janosik and his men. Some people said that he was a giant, and as strong as a hundred men. Others said that he was magic, that he could make himself invisible.

Duke Edmund grew more and more angry. He sent soldiers out by day and by night, but they couldn't find Janosik or his hidden camp. The Duke doubled the reward that he said he'd give anyone who turned Janosik in. But no one wanted it. His spies came to him with reports that many poor villagers were talking in secret and saying that there was about to be a rebellion. The people had had enough of Duke Edmund. They were secretly getting ready to fight him.

The Duke was mad with anger and worry. He went to get help from a witch who lived in the forest near his castle. The witch was a plump woman with a big wart on her chin. She told the Duke to come and sit with her in her filthy hut. After he'd paid her seven silver coins, the witch threw sand into a pan of water, and stared at it.

"What can you see?" asked Duke Edmund.

"I can see you will never catch Janosik while he has the gifts that the Spirits of the Mountain gave to him," the witch replied.

The Duke kicked over the pan of sand and water. "You must be able to do something!" he said. "Cast a spell on Janosik, so that he goes mad, and throws the gifts away!"

The witch shook her head. "I am only a witch," she said. "The magic of the Mountain Spirits is far more powerful than my magic."

Duke Edmund left the witch's hut, and rode off towards his castle. Four guards rode behind him, all armed with crossbows. Near the edge of the forest, a man with a ragged cloak stepped onto the road and blocked their way. His hood was pulled down to hide his face.

"Stand aside, beggar!" said Duke Edmund. "I'd let my horse trample you, but I don't want its hooves to get dirty!"

The man bowed low. "Tell me, my lord, what would you give me if I told you where Janosik is?" he said.

"The reward for Janosik is 200 gold coins," said the Duke.

"Janosik is not worth that much!" the beggar said. "Give me that fat purse you are carrying, and I will tell you where to find him."

The Duke took the purse from his belt, and threw it at the man's feet. The man bent down, picked up the purse, and put it in a pocket inside his cloak.

"Well?" snapped Duke Edmund. "Tell me – where is Janosik?"

The beggar pulled back his hood, and grinned at the Duke. "Here I am, my lord!" he said.

The Duke's eyes shone bright and evil. "Guards!" he called out. "Shoot him!"

The guards lifted their cross-bows and fired. Three arrows bounced off Janosik's magic clothes. He caught the fourth arrow with his left hand. "You will have to shoot better than that!" he said.

The guards charged at Janosik, but he was wearing his magic belt. He was off in a flash, and left nothing behind him but a cloud of dust.

The Duke's face turned purple with anger.

Chapter 7
The Traitor

That night, the bandits had a huge party in a village. There was plenty of food and drink, and it was all paid for with the money from Duke Edmund's purse. A bonfire blazed in the village square, and pipers and fiddlers played. People danced and sang.

Janosik spotted a pretty young girl in the crowd, and he went over to her. "What's your name?" he asked.

"Magda," she told him.

"Will you dance with me, Magda?" said Janosik.

Magda giggled. "You can dance with any girl here!" she said. "They're all longing to dance with you."

"Perhaps they are, but you're the one I've chosen," said Janosik.

Magda and Janosik danced around the bonfire. Light from the flames flashed in Magda's eyes as Janosik whirled her up into the air.

Nearby, a young man called Stefan stood sulking in the shadows. Stefan's friend Marek passed by, and stopped to speak to him.

"Hey, Stefan!" said Marek. "Is that your sweetheart Magda I see dancing with Janosik?"

"Magda is not my sweetheart!" Stefan said.

"No, but I bet you wish that she was!" Marek went on. "You'd better forget about her, my friend. She'll have nothing to do with you now that she's danced with Janosik!"

"Shut up, you fool!" said Stefan, but he knew that what Marek had said was true.

Stefan felt sick with anger and jealousy. He turned, and walked away from the village square. He didn't care where he went. When he got to the edge of the village, his anger had gone, but his jealousy was still strong.

The sound of loud snores made Stefan turn his head. He saw the two bandits whose job it was to keep watch in case Duke Edmund's soldiers attacked. They'd drunk far too much wine, and were fast asleep.

"I know!" Stefan muttered to himself. "I'll go to the Duke right now, and betray Janosik. The Duke will give me the reward money. Then I will be rich and I can get myself a sweetheart who is ten times prettier than Magda!"

Without another thought, he ran off into the night.

Chapter 8
The Spy's Plan

While Janosik and his men were busy feasting and dancing, Duke Edmund was in the hall of his castle. He sat at the long table. One of his spies was talking to him, and the Duke didn't like what the man was telling him.

"More people are turning against you every day, my lord," said the spy. "Many say that if Janosik led them, they'd be happy to fight to get rid of you."

"They wouldn't dare!" Duke Edmund said. "Those cowards! No one stands a chance against my soldiers. My men would cut them to pieces."

The spy spoke in a low voice. "My lord," he said, "I'm afraid that I've even heard some of your soldiers say that they'd rather follow Janosik than you."

The Duke thumped the table with his fist. "Janosik!" he growled. "That man is everywhere I turn. Everything was fine until he came along. The people used to pay their rents and taxes, and did as they were told. Now they're plotting against me, and it's all because of Janosik. They love a common thief more than they love me." A wild look came into the Duke's eyes. "Very well!" he went on. "If the people do not love me, then I must teach them how to fear me. I will hang and kill every last farmer in the Tatra Mountains!"

"It would be much simpler just to kill Janosik, my lord," said the spy. "Without him, the poor would obey you again. Janosik gives them something to hope for and makes them feel strong."

"I agree," Duke Edmund said. "But how can I hang a man when I can't find him? Trying to catch Janosik is like trying to catch a shadow."

Just then, a soldier marched Stefan into the hall.

"Excuse me, my lord," said the soldier. "This man says he has important news for you."

The Duke looked quickly at Stefan, and said, "Well? Out with it, man!"

"Janosik and his gang are in my village," Stefan said. "They're all drunk. They're having a huge party but the men on watch have fallen asleep. I can take you and your soldiers there."

For a moment, the Duke's face wore a happy smile, then he scowled. "What's the point?" he said with a sigh. "Even if we take Janosik by surprise, he will use his magic gifts to escape. You don't get a reward for just telling us where Janosik is. I want him handed over!"

The spy scratched his chin in a thoughtful way. "May I say something, my lord?" he said. "I know how you can catch Janosik even with his magic gifts."

"How?" asked the Duke.

"Order your soldiers to make a big circle round the village," said the spy. "Then tell Janosik that if he does not come out and give himself up, the villagers will all be killed."

"What if he refuses and then gets away?" Duke Edmund said.

"Then the villagers will die," replied the spy. "And that will be Janosik's fault. No one will think he's a hero any more. He will be the most hated man in Poland."

The Duke burst out laughing, and his laughter rang out around the hall.

Chapter 9
Captured

In the village, the party was over. The bonfire burned low, and the music was silent. Most of the villagers had gone home to bed. Janosik had danced his last dance with Magda, and was talking to Leon in the village square.

"Shall I gather the men together?" asked Leon.

"No," said Janosik, yawning. "Let them rest. We will leave for our camp in the forest at first light."

Leon saw an odd look on his leader's face. "Is something wrong, Janosik?" he said.

Janosik gave a shrug. "Since I was a small boy, I've had to keep moving on from place to place, always running, always hiding. Tonight made me think how nice it would be to settle down and live a peaceful life."

Janosik and Leon heard the thudding of horses' hooves, and the jingling of harnesses. Who could it be? Then Duke Edmund rode into the square, with his soldiers on either side of him. "The village is surrounded," the Duke told Janosik. "Give yourself up to me, or I will order my men to kill the villagers."

"Don't listen to him, Janosik!" muttered Leon. "It's a trick."

"I can't afford to take that risk, my friend," said Janosik. He turned to the Duke, and said, "Very well, I surrender."

The Duke's mouth twisted into a cruel smile. "You won't be needing your magic clothes and staff any more, Janosik. Onto the fire with them!"

Janosik did as he was told, and threw his jacket, shirt, belt, boots and staff onto the bonfire. There was a flash of bright blue light, and the gifts were gone.

"Seize him, men!" said Duke Edmund.

"Shall I fetch a rope to hang him with, my lord?" one of the guards said.

"I'm not going to hang him yet," said Duke Edmund. "First I will force poor people from every village in the mountains to my castle. Then I will hang Janosik in front of them. That will show them that I am their master."

Janosik was locked away in the Duke's dark prison. He looked through the iron bars of the cell window, down into the courtyard of the castle. For two days, he watched carpenters saw and hammer as they built the gallows on which he would be hung.

Though Janosik felt afraid, he made up his mind not to show his fear. "I will go to my death like a brave man, not like a coward," he promised himself.

On the morning of the third day, two soldiers came to Janosik's cell. They tied his hands behind his back, and led him outside.

Chapter 10
On the Gallows

The courtyard was crowded with poor people. Duke Edmund was waiting on the gallows with the hangman, who wore a black mask. Soldiers with cross-bows kept watch on the crowd. Everyone fell silent when they saw Janosik, except for an old woman who stood near the foot of the gallows. She had a shawl over her head, and her nose was deep in a large red handkerchief. "Poor Janosik!" she sobbed. "Poor boy!"

The two soldiers marched Janosik onto the gallows, then went to stand with the other soldiers at the edge of the crowd.

Duke Edmund stepped forward. "People of the mountains!" he began. "This man Janosik is guilty of a crime far worse than theft. He thought that I, your Duke, should not rule over you, and he filled your minds with false promises of freedom. Today, he will die, and those promises will die with him."

The old woman with the red handkerchief sobbed even louder. "Poor Janosik!" she wailed. "Poor, poor boy!"

The Duke was angry that the stupid old woman was spoiling his fine speech. "Be quiet, old hag!" he roared.

Before anyone could stop her, the old woman jumped up onto the gallows. She took a sword from under her skirt, slashed through Janosik's bonds, handed him the sword, and pushed the hangman to the floor. As she wrestled, her shawl fell off. She was Leon in disguise!

"People of the mountains, you have long dreamed of freedom!" shouted Janosik. "Now is the time to fight for it!"

The rest of Janosik's gang were among the crowd. They had swords and daggers hidden in their clothes, and they gave them out to the villagers, who attacked the Duke's soldiers. Some brave villagers died in the fight, but most of the soldiers were taken by surprise, and were knocked to the ground before they could even strike a blow.

Duke Edmund pulled out his sword and ran at Janosik. Again and again their blades clashed together, the steel glinting in the morning sunshine. The Duke slashed at Janosik's legs. The robber leapt over the blade. The Duke brought his sword up in a deadly curve. Janosik jumped away and grabbed the dangling rope noose that was there to hang him. He held onto it and swung at the Duke. The point of Janosik's sword pierced his enemy's heart, and Duke Edmund fell dead.

The fighting did not last long after the Duke died. Most of the soldiers put down their swords and cross-bows, and surrendered.

The people were over-joyed. They wanted to cheer Janosik, and carry him on their shoulders, but when they looked for him, they couldn't find him anywhere.

****

There are different stories about what had happened to Janosik afterwards. No one knows which is true. In one story, Janosik crept back to the village, married Magda, had a family, and lived the rest of his life in peace.

Another story says that the Spirits of the Mountain used their powers to fly Janosik off to their secret cave, and put him into a magic sleep. He is still sleeping there now, but if ever the freedom of the people in the Tatra Mountains is in danger, Janosik will wake up, and lead them to victory.

BATTLE CARDS

Andrew Matthews

Author

Favourite hero:
Theseus.

Favourite monster:
The Dragon.

Your weapon of choice:
A Samurai sword.

Special secret power:
Being able to fly.

Favourite fight scene:
The battle between Herakles and the Hydra.

Goodie or baddie:
I would be the baddie – baddies seem to have more fun.

RELOADED

WHO WILL WIN?

Dylan Gibson

Illustrator

Favourite hero:
Captain Kirk from Star Trek.

Favourite monster:
I love the creatures in the film Pan's Labyrinth.

Your weapon of choice:
Maybe magic powers? I wouldn't want to get up close and personal with a sword or axe.

Special secret power:
I read a lot of science books and bore people to sleep with facts.

Goodie or baddie:
Good, in real life. Bad guys always have more fun in books or in film though!

R
E
L
O
A
D
E
D

Barrington Stoke would like to thank all its readers for commenting on the manuscript before publication and in particular:

Ikra Ahmed
Afshan Akhtar
Aseeba Azher
Theresa Bird
Charlotte Booth
Jean Button
Misbah Chaudhry
Dominic Dougherty
Lee Forbes
Sebastian Gijsbers
Jason Gill
Lauren Gormlie
Thomas Gregory-Coles
Cherise Grubey
Joanne Hart
Shane Hazelwood
Oliver Hemmings

Thomas Honeybell
Tino Mano
Catherie McAlpine
Arron Monaghan
Yannick Nziza
Newsha Parastaran
Savita Rathor
James Simpson
Sabah Tahir
Sara
Simon
Zayna Tahseen
Sophie Venables
Carol Williams
V. Woodward

Become a Consultant!

Would you like to give us feedback on our titles before they are published? Contact us at the email address below – we'd love to hear from you!

info@barringtonstoke.co.uk
www.barringtonstoke.co.uk